Published in Great Britain in MMXXII by
Scribblers, an imprint of
The Salariya Book Company Ltd
25 Marlborough Place, Brighton BN1 1UB
www.salariya.com

ISBN: 978-1-913337-93-3

© The Salariya Book Company Ltd MMXXII
All rights reserved. No part of this publication may be reproduced, stored in or introduced into a retrieval system or transmitted in any form, or by any means (electronic, mechanical, photocopying, recording or otherwise) without the written permission of the publisher. Any person who does any unauthorised act in relation to this publication may be liable to criminal prosecution and civil claims for damages.

1 3 5 7 9 8 6 4 2

A CIP catalogue record for this book is available from the British Library.

This book is sold subject to the conditions that it shall not, by way of trade or otherwise, be lent, resold, hired out, or otherwise circulated without the publisher's prior consent in any form or binding or cover other than that in which it is published and without similar condition being imposed on the subsequent purchaser.

Editor: Nick Pierce

Visit
www.salariya.com
for our online catalogue and
free fun stuff.

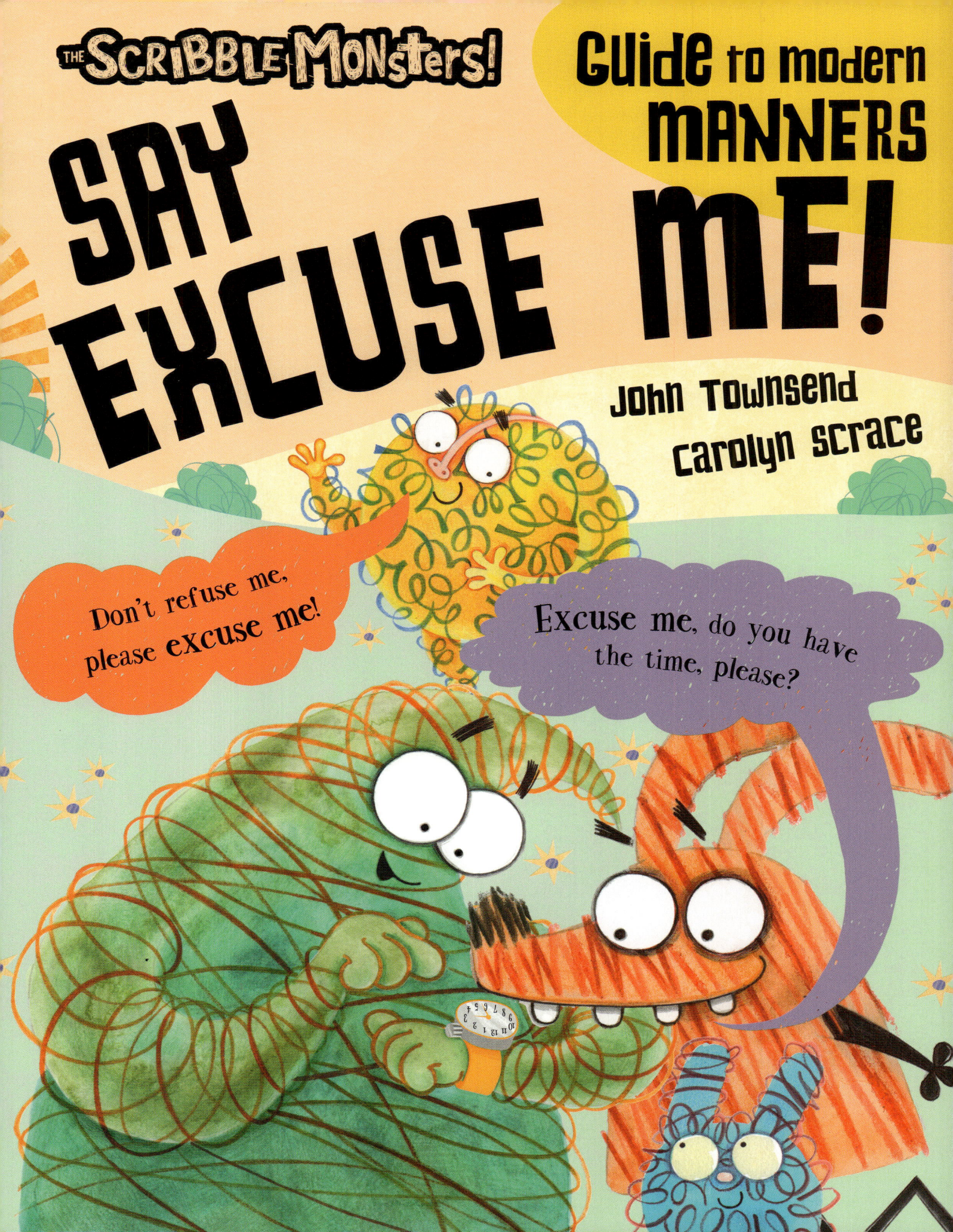

Some little children can forget
To leave kind words behind them...
We're here to scribble our advice
And find ways to remind them.

Think of others

Excuse me please!

Monsters with manners

Good manners show you care

Be polite

'Excuse Me' are two words that show
You're giving others thought.
Showing manners is a pleasure,
Is what my grandma taught.

Excuse me, do you have the time, please?

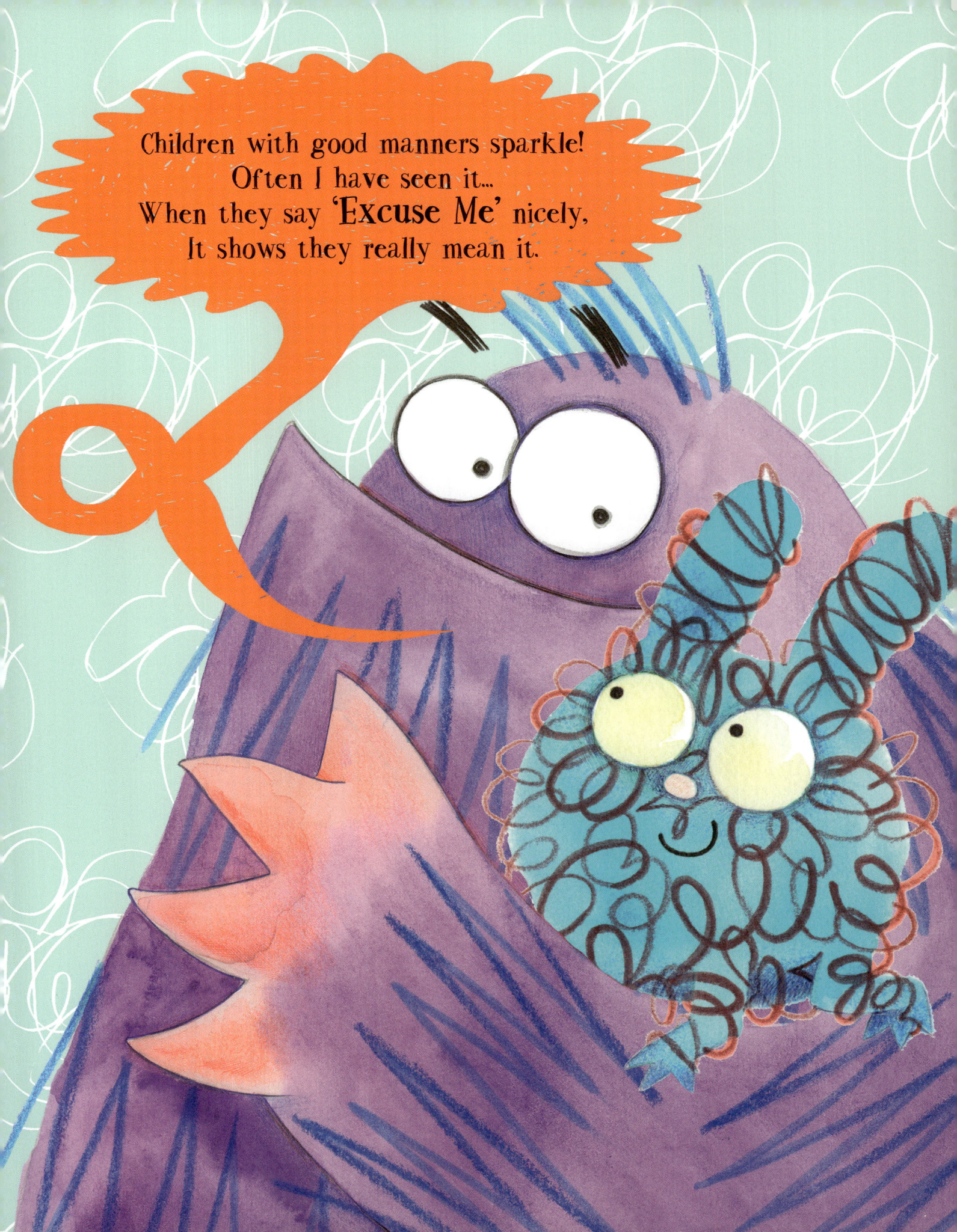

H.B. tries to leave the table,
It's such a squash and squeeze.
Without a fuss, the right words are

Will you **Excuse Me**, please?

It's not polite to interrupt
While other people talk,
But Nibs needs help and has to ask
For a plate, a knife and fork.

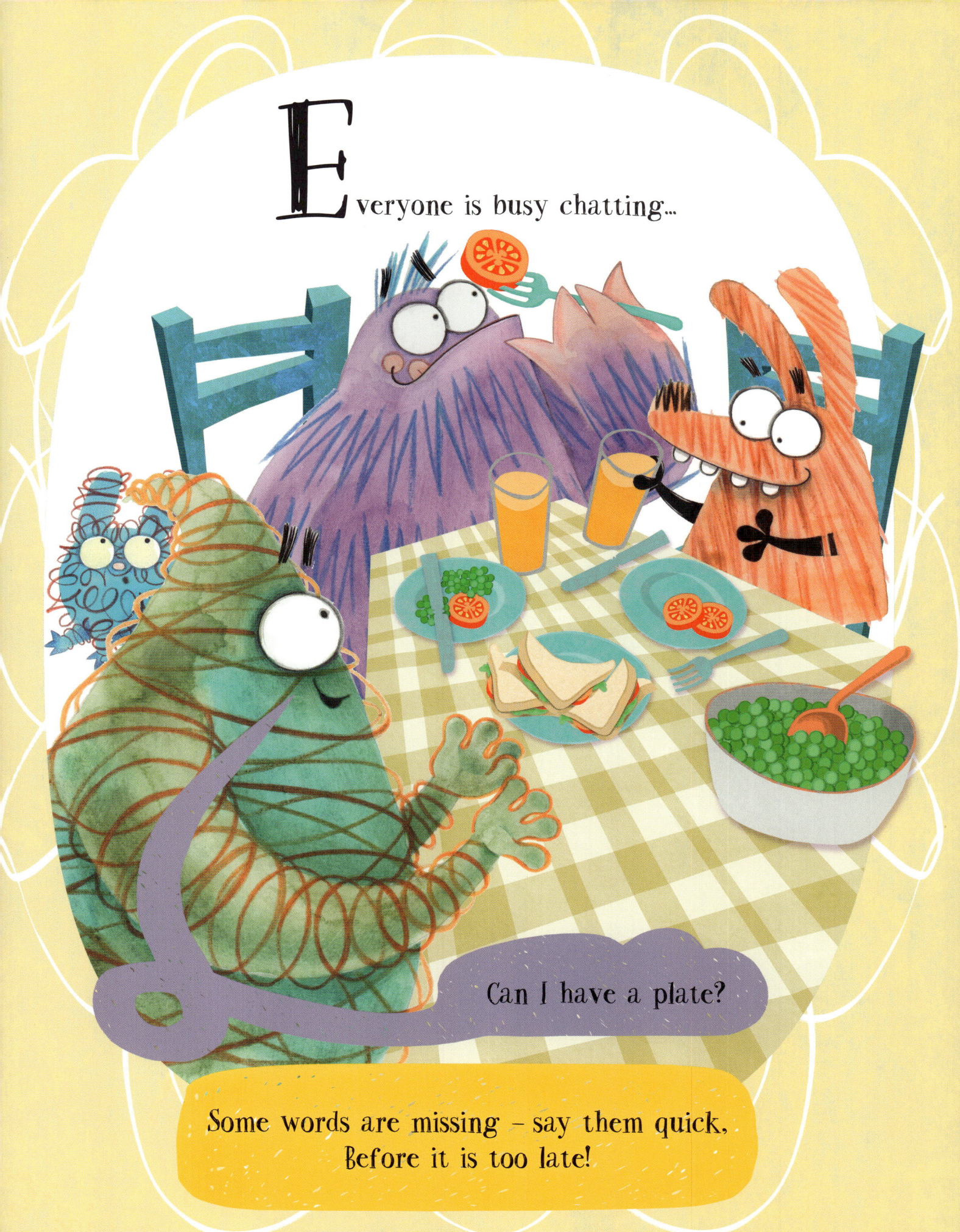

'Excuse Me' is the proper way
To get a crowd's attention.
Pablo says it in the dentist's,
Then,

There's something I must mention...

Inky stretches over others
To reach a pile of books...
No **'Excuse Me'** brings big grumbles
And lots of grumpy looks.

H.B. does the same politely,
With first a friendly call:

I'm sorry – do Excuse Me, please.

Then no one minds at all!

Children who remember manners
And don't forget **'Excuse Us'**
Make the Scribble Monsters thrilled...

Oh, how you so enthuse us!

CAN YOU HELP US FIND THE ANSWERS TO THIS QUIZ...

QUESTION 1

What do I say when my tummy rumbles?

QUESTION 2

We give awards to children who say what two words?

MORE MONSTER QUESTIONS

QUESTION 5

When I asked 'can I have a plate', what words were missing?

QUESTION 6

Should I shout 'Hey listen to me!' when I need to get everyone's attention?

QUESTION 7

What should I say when I can't stop yawning?

QUESTION 8

What do we all do when we hear you say 'Excuse Me'?

Look at the last page of the book to see if you are right!